For Brett:
Best brother, best friend.

Capybara Is Friends with Everyone
Copyright © 2022 by Maddie Frost
Written and illustrated by Maddie Frost
All rights reserved. Manufactured in Italy. No part of this book may be used or reproduced in any manner whatsoever
without written permission except in the case of brief quotations embodied in critical articles and reviews.
For information address HarperCollins Children's Books, a division of HarperCollins Publishers, 195 Broadway, New York, NY 10007.
www.harpercollins.com

ISBN 978-0-06-302102-0

Typography by Chelsea C. Donaldson
The artist used Adobe Photoshop to create the digital illustrations for this book.
21 22 23 24 25   RTLO   10 9 8 7 6 5 4 3 2 1
❖
First Edition

CAPYBARA IS FRIENDS WITH EVERYONE

RESERVED

Maddie Frost

HARPER
An Imprint of HarperCollinsPublishers

Being a great friend
means going above
and beyond.

Take it from me—I have **4,382** friends.

It's important my friends always know I'm here for them . . .

Which is why I start each day with an announcement.

Then I spring into action.

I will do anything for my friends.
Their convenience is my number one concern.

"Grabbed your lunch!"

"Got your mail!"

"Watered your plants!"

Isn't that right . . . Um . . .

This calls for my super special
Capybara NEW FRIEND song!

Hi, hello, new friend.
My name is Capybara.
I'm gonna jump and cheer-a.

It's such a happy day.
The happiest days of days.
There is no better day
Because I met you today.
HOORAY!

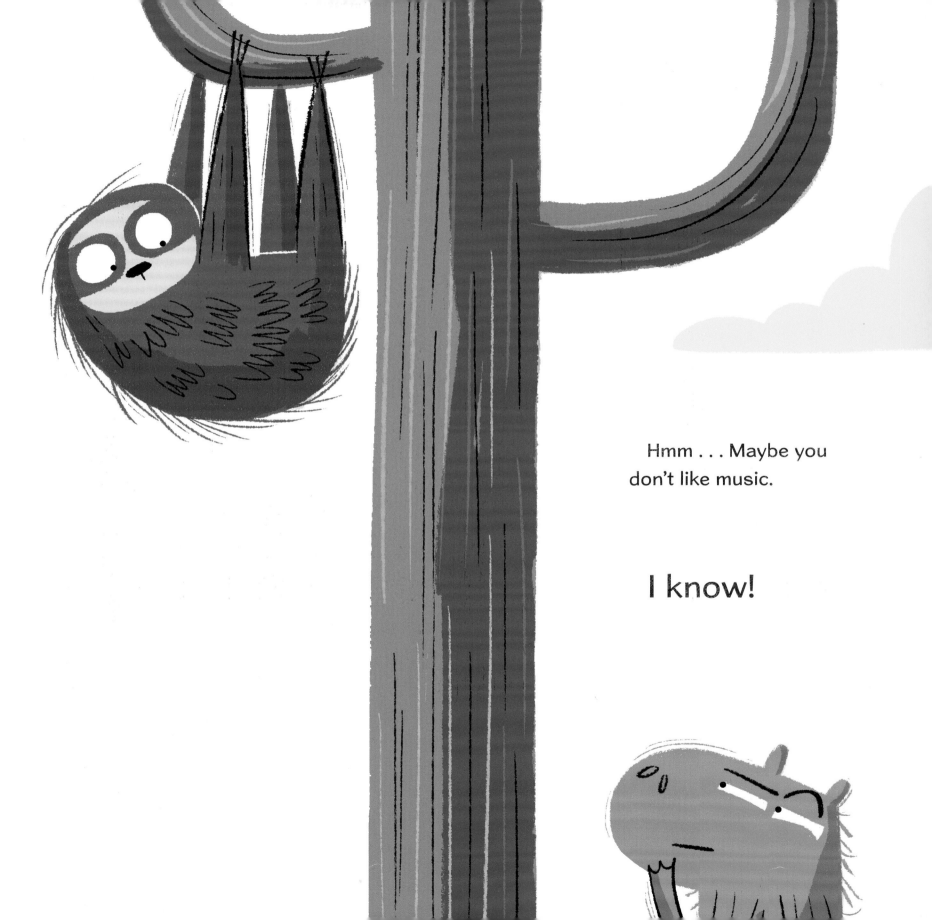

Hmm . . . Maybe you
don't like music.

I know!

How about flowers?

Or a Bundt cake?

A gift basket full of bathtime essentials?

POP

What about a mosaic?

Or a Zen garden?

I carved you a statue with
my little webbed feet!

Whaddaya say?

Friends?

I don't understand.
Is it me?
Is it something I said?

Are my webbed feet too webby?

That's OK. No problemo.
It's not like I need to be
friends with EVERYONE.

Here I am just walking away, not bothered at all.
Dum-dee-dum, what a lovely day.

PLEASE BE MY FRIEND!

I can make you a better . . .

Zen . . .

. . . garden.

Let me know what you need!

I'll be right—yawwwwwn—

Here.

"I just nnnne-e-e-e-e-edddded to get my-y-y-y-y-y-y-y-y-y-y-y kazzzzzzzzzzo-o-o-o-o-o-o-o-o-o-o-o for the new-w-w-w-w friend so-o-o-o-ong."

Oh.
I see.

OH, I SEE!!!

And all this time I thought—
That you just—
Which means—

You really ARE my friend!

Does anyone have a leaf?
THE TEARS OF JOY ARE COMING!

Being a great friend means going above and beyond.
But not *all the time.*
Sometimes it means doing less.

"Got you a basket to carry your twigs."

"I'm at the best part, but there are ants back that way."

ME TIME

"How does half a block sound? I'm meeting my friend Sloth."

And sometimes being a great friend just means hanging out.

It's such a happy day.
The happiest days of days.

"Take it away, Sloth!"

"Zoot-ah-zoot-ah-zoo"

And **sometimes** it means doing nothing at all.

THANK YOU, CAPYBARA!
SLOTH MONKEY JAGUAR The Anteaters Tapir
The Turtles
Toucan Lemur ORANGUTAN CROCODILE Blue Bird Panther
SSSNAKE Okapi Frog PINK BIRD LIZARD

Take it from me—I have **4,383** friends!